DAISY MAY
Goes Out to Play

Britton Taylor

PAGE PUBLISHING
Conneaut Lake, PA

First originally published by Page Publishing 2023

ISBN 979-8-88654-727-6 (pbk)
ISBN 979-8-88654-737-5 (digital)

Printed in the United States of America

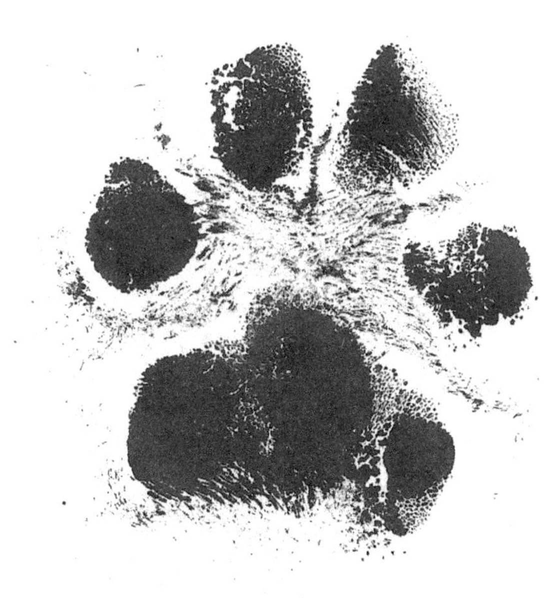

The weather was warm with a very soft breeze. The sun lit up the day with the greatest of ease. The sky was blue with a very light sheen, and up in the trees, a black bird was seen.

Then came Daisy May, with her fur coat of yellow, to meet the young bird and just say hello. She barked, "I'm Daisy May, and I am a dog. Come meet my friend, Herm. He's a green frog."

The bird said with a caw, "Nice to meet you, Daisy May. I am a crow. My friends call me Jay."

Off the pair went to Herm's lily pad, and on the way there, what a fun time was had. She ran, and he flew. They laughed and they played until they came to the pond where little Herm stayed.

Daisy May said, "Herm, meet our new friend, Jay. He's a very nice crow. We've come over to play."

"A pleasure to meet you," said the kindhearted crow. "I can't wait to watch our new friendship grow."

"Here's to our trio," Herm the Frog croaked then hopped in the water, and they all got soaked. Although he was tiny, Herm made a big splash, then Daisy May jumped in with Jay in a flash. They played in the water then headed toward town.

On the path was a dog whose fur coat was brown. Daisy May was tall, while the brown dog was short, and to the group of chums, he had this to report. "I'll be a great friend," he barked, "if you give me a chance. I am Sir Lancelot Horatio, but you can call me Lance."

"Why, hello there, Lance. My name's Daisy May. This here is Herm, and over there is Jay. We're headed to town, if you'd like to come too. We'll all be best friends when this day is through."

So the foursome set out on the path into town, each cutting up and being a clown. Playing some games and scampering along, doing a little dance, and singing a song.

Then a red squirrel came out of nowhere. She squeaked and squeaked to announce she was there. They all said hello and gave her their names then asked if she'd like to join in their games. "Why, of course, I would" is what she replied. "I heard you all singing, and I've never tried. I love to play games, just dance, and be silly. Let's all be friends. My name is Tilly."

The group now at five, they kept on the trail. Moving fast as lightning then slow as a snail. Hooting and hollering and whistling a tune, with smiles on their faces as big as the moon.

Daisy May spoke up, "I have a treat. When we get into town, there's someone to meet. She is a cat, and we're really tight. I call her Snowball because her fur is snow white."

They walked over a hill and right into town, all shaking things up and getting down. Scooting along, excited to meet their new companion who lived down the street. They came to a house, and there was no hunt. The super nice cat was lounging out front. Daisy May introduced the fun-loving bunch and said, "We'll all be pals. I have a hunch."

"I'm glad you're all here," she meowed. "My name is Pat. It's short for Patricia, but I don't like that. Just call me Snowball like Miss Daisy May. Let's go have a blast on this beautiful day."

All six of the buddies skipped to the park, to romp with each other, before it got dark. They ran through the fields and played hide-and-seek, then Tilly the Squirrel let out a big shriek.

Out from the grass came a coldhearted snake. He hissed his remark, "What's this, for Pete's sake? Dogs, cats, and birds don't get along. With a squirrel and a frog, this is just wrong! Some of you are big, while some of you small, and you're all different colors. You don't match at all. There should be fighting, calling everyone names, not singing and dancing and playing these games. There's nothing in common. It just isn't right. Where's the prejudice, anger, hatred, and spite? It's all very alarming and so easy to see that all six of you are not meant to be."

Daisy May wasn't pleased with this hateful speech. She scorned the cruel snake and had these words to preach: "We have one thing in common. We're all creatures of Earth, each unique and special with value and worth. I really don't care, black, white, or brown. They make me smile, but you make me frown. It doesn't matter, red, yellow, or green. We are all friends, and you are just mean. I cannot tolerate beliefs such as this or the poisonous venom in the words that you hiss. So slither on, snake. We don't share that view. You're a big dummy. I feel sorry for you!"

Then she barked and growled to chase him away, and the gang all cheered, shouting, "Hip hip hooray! She is our hero, and she's got it right. We should have fun and play, not argue and fight. On the inside we're all the same, so come on, everyone, let's finish our game."

And they played hide-and-seek the rest of the day until our hero had these words to say: "We all should head home. It's getting late, but we'll play again. I really can't wait."

They all shared some hugs and said their goodbyes, then Daisy May went home with joy in her eyes. She made some new friends, and they played all day even though they were different in most every way.

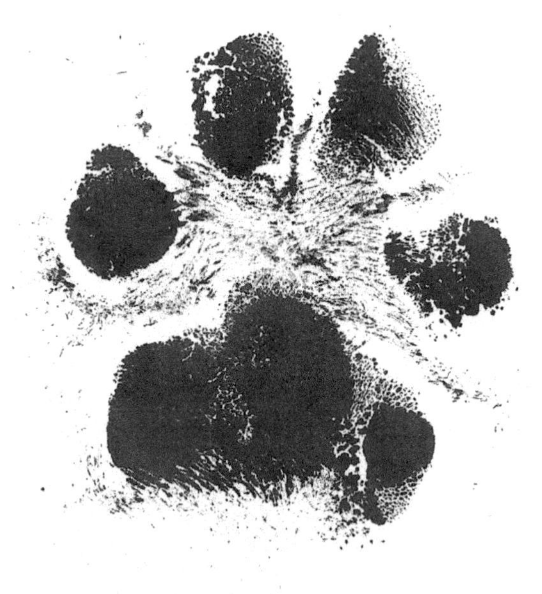

The sky turned dark, and the stars shone bright when sweet Daisy May, she said, "Good night."

HAPPY
BIRTHDAY

About the Author

Britton Taylor is a short-story writer with aspirations of being a novelist. He lives in Las Vegas, Nevada, with his sweet Labrador, Daisy May. Besides spending time with her, he enjoys snowboarding, watching documentaries, and rooting for his beloved sports teams—Go Cowboys, Rockets, Astros, VGK, and Runnin Rebels! Mr. Taylor wanted to share what a beautiful and loving soul Daisy May is and felt a children's book would be the best way to convey that. Daisy May is an exceptionally special dog, and Mr. Taylor is certain that the world will love her just as much as he does.

www.ingramcontent.com/pod-product-compliance
Lightning Source LLC
Chambersburg PA
CBHW040205160726
48006CB00014B/1910